For Tony and Robina – thanks for the life raft! J.D.

Text copyright © Jan Dean 1999
Illustrations copyright © Tony Kerins 1999

First published in Great Britain in 1999
by Macdonald Young Books
an imprint of Wayland Publishers Ltd
61 Western Road
Hove
East Sussex
BN3 1JD

Find Macdonald Young Books on the internet at
http://www.myb.co.uk

Designed and Typeset by Don Martin
Printed in Hong Kong by Wing King Tong Co. Ltd.

British Library Cataloguing in Publication Data available

ISBN: 0 7500 2702 9 (pb)

Jan Dean

The
Claygate Hound

Illustrated by Tony Kerins

Macdonald Young Books

Chapter One

Every year, Class Six at Malham Primary
went to Claygate for school camp. It was
fantastic. There was a farm, an adventure
playground and best of all, Claygate Wood,
a wonderful, mysterious place to explore.

When they arrived Class Six was buzzing with excitement.

Ryan and Zeb climbed down from the bus and looked around.

"Cool!" Ryan said. "Let's explore."

"Not so fast, you two," Mr Weston, their teacher, called. "Unpack first."

Chatting and joking, Class Six boys hurried to their bunk room. Ryan and Zeb raced ahead and grabbed a bunk by the window.

They tossed for the top bunk. Zeb won.

"You can see all the way to the woods from here," he said.

"Trust you two to get the best bunks," Martin Davis complained.

"Tough," Ryan said. "We were here first."

Billy Dunmore climbed on to Zeb's bunk and sat beside him. "I wouldn't sleep here," he said.

"Why not?" Zeb asked.

"Too near the woods."

"So?"

"*So*, the Claygate Hound might come and get you!"

"The *what*?"

"It's a ghost dog. It has huge fangs and mad red eyes. It haunts Claygate Woods. Look!"

Zeb stared. Something was moving amongst the trees – a dark shadowy shape.

"That's it!" Billy hissed. "And if we can see it – it can see us. I wouldn't sleep this near the window. Not even if you paid me!"

The chatter in the bunk room died away. Everyone was listening now. Billy smiled. He liked frightening people. He told them scary stories to make them nervous. Then he laughed at them and called them chicken or scaredy-cat.

"Shut up, Dunmore," Ryan snapped. "It could be anything out there. It's not your stupid ghost dog. You made that up."

"I did not. There *is* a hound. My brother was here last year. He told me all about it."

"Oh yeah?" Zeb folded his arms and looked bored. Freezing Billy out was the only way to make him leave you alone.

But Billy just grinned. "I'll wait till tonight. Then I'll tell you all about it."

"Don't bother," Ryan said. "We don't want to know."

Just then the door opened and Sally Palmer peered in.

"Oi!" Martin shouted. "No girls in here!"

"Mr Weston sent me. It's time for tea," Sally announced.

"Come on, Zeb," Ryan said. "I'm starving."

Chapter Two

At tea they met Granny Hatcher. She lived in Claygate Farm. She was thin and spindly with grey hair. Ryan thought she looked rather like a scarecrow – as if she'd been made out of old broom-handles.

She served them steaming bowls of home-made soup and thick slices of fresh-baked bread and butter. It was delicious.

"Apple pie and custard," Zeb whispered, when he saw pudding. "I think I must have died and gone to heaven!"

Across the table Billy Dunmore gave a sour laugh. "People who die in Claygate don't get to heaven," he said.

"Give it a rest, Dunmore," Ryan snapped. "We know what you're going to say: the horrible Claygate Hound gets them. Right?"

Billy grinned like a hyena. "What's the matter, Ryan? Am I getting to you?"

"No!"

"Poor old Ryan," Billy went on. "Away from home and scared of ghosts..."

"Shut it, Dunmore," Zeb said. "Or I'll..."

"Or you'll what?"

Everyone at the table was watching.

Mr Weston was at the other end of their table.

"Or you'll what?" Billy asked again.

"You want to watch it, young man," a soft country voice said. "Our hound don't like being talked about.

Startled, the boys looked round. Behind them stood Granny Hatcher. She stared hard at Billy. Her eyes shone like black diamonds.

"If he hears you, he might come and get you. So, if I was you, I'd eat a bit more and say a bit less."

Then she smiled at Zeb. "Was it you that admired my pie?"

Zeb nodded enthusiastically.

"Have another slice, dear. Tuck in. I like to see a lad enjoy his food."

Chapter Three

"Weird, or what?" Zeb said after tea. "Do you think Granny Hatcher's scary? It was spooky the way she just *knew* what was going on."

"I expect she overheard," Ryan said sensibly.

"Didn't you think that stuff about the hound was creepy?"

"It was great," Ryan said. "It's about time somebody scared Billy Dunmore. Come on, let's check out the adventure playground."

It was amazing. There was a mini assault course, a whole jungle of scramble-nets and platforms in the trees.

Mr Weston set a challenge. He put a bag of chocolate bars right in the centre of the nets, then split the class into two teams –

girls against boys. Each team started from opposite ends of the course. The first team to get all its members to the chocolate got to eat the winnings.

The girls won.

"Not fair," Martin complained. "It was easier from their end!"

"Rubbish," Mr Weston said. "They won fair and square."

Zeb and Ryan loved the nets. They stayed there until dark. Everyone else had gone inside. Then, a cold, unearthly moan rose from the woods and echoed in the darkness. Suddenly the playground did not feel safe. The nets cast sinister shadows and the trees shivered in the wind, dark and forbidding.

Ryan and Zeb looked at each other. What if Billy was right? What if the dark shape they had seen running through the trees really was a ghost dog? They scrambled down from their platform and hurried back indoors.

Chapter Four

Lights out was at ten, but the boys were too excited to sleep. Martin ran round pulling duvets off the bunks. Soon a full-scale pillow battle was underway.

"Enough!" Mr Weston's face was like thunder.

Finally the boys settled. Ryan reached under his pillow and felt for his lucky tin. It looked like junk – all battered and scratched with a huge dent in the lid. But it was very special indeed. It had once belonged to his grandad – and it had saved his life.

Grandad had been a soldier in the war. He had carried this old tin in his breast pocket.

Once it had stopped a bullet. The dent was where the bullet had bounced off the tin. If the tin hadn't been there, the bullet would have gone straight into Grandad's heart.

It had been Grandad's lucky tin and now it was Ryan's. He kept it with him all the time. It was his most precious thing.

He was almost asleep when Billy started to whisper. "There *is* a ghost dog... an enormous hound... its eyes are like fire and its howl can freeze your blood. And whoever sees it is doomed..."

Ryan's heart beat faster. He gripped his lucky tin tightly. He knew it was stupid to let Billy scare him, but the unearthly howling from the woods echoed in his memory.

There was *something* out there.

Zeb remembered the howling too. "Shut up, Dunmore, we're trying to sleep," he snapped.

"Yeah," Martin agreed. "I'm whacked. Put a sock in it."

But Billy went on, "If you see the Claygate Hound, you *die*," he said and gave an evil chuckle. "It roams the woods looking for its next victim. And whoever sees it *dies... horribly...*"

What if Billy's right? Ryan wondered. Why am I the one who saw it in the trees? Why am I the one who keeps hearing it? What if it's coming to get me?

Outside the trees creaked and moaned. The wind was rising. Above its wild swishing, Ryan was sure he could hear a ghostly howl.

Chapter Five

It was funny how lessons didn't seem so bad when you weren't in a classroom. Everyone worked so hard that Mr Weston gave them extra free time. Ryan and Zeb decided to spend it exploring Claygate Woods.

No one else chose the woods. Being alone made them feel more adventurous – like real explorers.

Dozens of small paths wound through the trees.

"It's like a maze," Ryan said.

"Let's cut through here." Zeb pointed to a shadowy gap in the bushes.

In his pocket Ryan rubbed his tin for luck. "OK," he said. "Let's go for it."

They pushed through the undergrowth until they reached a clearing. In the middle was a tumble-down ruin. Most of the walls were just rubble, but one still stood tall. It was covered with dark green ivy. There were plenty of footholds and handholds.

"Cool," Ryan said. "Let's climb!"

They grabbed handfuls of ivy but it pulled away from the crumbling stone. Showers of grit fell into their faces.

"Euch!" Ryan said. Then he fell silent.

Behind the ivy, on the old grey stone, was a faded painting – a picture of a huge, black dog.

It was the Claygate Hound. Ryan was sure of it. He remembered the strange, ghostly howling and his heart beat fast with fear. He shivered and stepped back, away from the wall.

The eyes of the painted hound glittered in the setting sun.

"It looks alive..." Ryan whispered.

Suddenly, the ground beneath his feet rumbled and from deep within the earth came an eerie cry – part wolf-howl, part dog-yelp.

"What is it?" Zeb gasped.

But they did not wait to find out.

Chapter Six

Back in the bunk room, they talked it over.
Had they really heard a ghost dog?

"No. It was a rush of air whooshing round
the ruins. That's all." Ryan said.

"It *sounded* like a dog," Zeb said.

"We were looking at a picture of a dog,"
Ryan explained. "So when we heard the
noise we thought it *was* a dog."

That made sense. Believing in ghostly
hounds when you were in a spooky place was
one thing. Believing in them in the safety of
the bunk room was just too silly for words.

That night, after lights out, Ryan felt
under his pillow for his lucky tin. It was not
there. Where could it be? He racked his
memory. Finally he realized. It was in the
woods. When they were running away from
the ruin, it must have fallen from his pocket.

He tossed and turned. That tin had been through a whole war – through all kinds of dangers. And now it was lost in Claygate Woods. He had to find it. He owed it to Grandad.

When he thought everyone was asleep, he slipped quietly out of bed and got dressed.

Sleepily, Zeb leaned over the top bunk. "What's the matter?"

"Sshh..." Ryan warned. "You'll wake everyone up."

Zeb rubbed his eyes. "What are you doing?"

"I'm going back to the woods."

"Now? You can't —"

"I have to, Zeb. I've lost my lucky tin and I just have to get it back."

"Then I'm coming with you," Zeb said.

In silence they crept past the sleeping boys. A few minutes later they were outside.

"Are you sure about this?" Zeb asked. "It's so dark... And what about the dog?"

"It was a trick echo," Ryan said as confidently as he could. "A *sound* mirage. And our imagination. If it wasn't for Billy we'd never have thought it was anything but the wind."

Zeb sighed. It wasn't just Billy, was it? It was Granny Hatcher and that weird picture underneath the ivy.

"I can't leave Grandad's tin out there," Ryan said stubbornly.

Zeb saw Ryan's determined face and he knew there was no point in arguing. "Come on, then," he said.

As they hurried into the trees, a strange, bony shadow flitted across the farmyard and followed them into the heart of the dark woods...

Chapter Seven

After the darkness under the trees, the moonlit clearing seemed very bright. The tumble-down stones of the ruin seemed to glow and the silvery light cast weird shadows on the painting of the black dog.

The boys hesitated. Neither of them wanted to go any closer. It looked too real, as if at any moment it might leap off the wall and come bounding after them.

It's just a painting, Ryan said to himself. Then, bravely, he stepped forwards.

There was his lucky tin, shining in the moonlight.

"Yes!" he yelled and he ran forward and grabbed it.

"Come on, Ryan," Zeb urged. "Let's get out of here."

"I've found it, Zeb," Ryan said. "I've got it back!" He could hardly believe it. He'd really worried about coming back here, but it had been so easy. Now he felt great – too great to believe in ghostly hounds.

I wonder who lived here? he thought as he stepped into the ruins.

As he set foot upon the ancient floor, the moonlit painting shimmered. A huge, black dog with glittering eyes and giant paws rose up out of the stones. It threw back its head and howled.

Ryan jumped back. There was a growling, rumbling sound and the great hound bared its teeth and snarled. They could see its gaping mouth, its sharp white teeth, its lolling red tongue. Ryan's eyes grew wide with terror. He stumbled backwards away from those dreadful jaws.

The rumbling deepened – like drums in the earth – and the ground beneath him trembled. Suddenly a jagged hole gaped at his feet like a bottomless pit. Soil and stones crashed down into it. Timbers slid and jolted, disappearing into the blackness.

This has been here all the time, Ryan thought in panic, hidden by rotten planks.

A second tremor struck and Ryan stumbled.

Then the dog leapt, its mad red eyes shining in the moonlight.

"Watch out!" Zeb shouted.

Ryan struggled to keep his balance – on the very brink of falling into the pit. Only his fear of the monstrous dog gave him the strength to jump clear.

"Run!" Zeb yelled.

But over the sliding stones and falling timbers the hound was coming for them…

Chapter Seven

Ryan and Zeb crashed through the bushes.
The hound was gaining on them. They
could hear the drum of its running feet, feel
its hot breath. Any second now it would be
on them, tearing them with those terrible
teeth...

Suddenly, they were
on the path. A figure
loomed up before
them. Behind them
was the ferocious
hound. There was
nowhere to turn.
Ryan screamed.

"Calm down," Granny Hatcher's soft voice soothed. "You're safe now."

In a panic Zeb blurted out the whole story. "...And now the hound is going to get us," he sobbed.

"Nonsense."

"But we saw it."

"I don't doubt that for a minute."

"Billy Dunmore said if you see the dog you die..."

Granny Hatcher sniffed. "That Dunmore boy's a menace."

"You said the dog would come and get Billy!"

"She said that to shut him up," Ryan said. "You know that."

Granny Hatcher smiled. "The dog appears to those in danger. He comes to warn. *If* you don't heed the warning *then* you might die. Foolish folk like Billy Dunmore get hold of the wrong end of the stick."

"But he looked so fierce," Zeb said, remembering the wild eyes and powerful body.

"The legend says that long ago the Claygate Hound let his master fall to his death. Then the poor old dog sat by his grave until he died too. It's not a story about a monster dog. It's a very sad story."

Granny Hatcher led them home.

"It took courage to rescue your grandad's tin," she said. "It must mean a lot to you."

Ryan nodded. "I nearly fell into that hole. I could have broken my neck."

"Very likely," Granny Hatcher said. "Old ruins have old cellars – very dangerous places. I expect you would have fallen, if something hadn't stopped you..."

Outside the wood, they turned and looked back into the shadows. In the distance a dark shape lurked, and a pair of faithful brown eyes glittered in the moonlight.

"Thank you," Ryan whispered.

From deep within the woods a single bark answered him.

DARE TO BE SCARED!

Are you brave enough to try more titles in the Tremors series? They're guaranteed to chill your spine...

The Curse of the Ghost Horse by Anthony Masters
Only Jake believes the eerie tale of Black Bess, a handsome black mare that fell to her death when she was forced to jump a huge crevasse. From that day, bad luck and Black Bess's ghost have haunted the area. Tormented by his father's illness, Jake is determined to jump the crevasse and find Black Bess. But will Jake's obsession lead to his death?

The Ghosts of Golfhawk School by Tessa Potter
Martin and Dan love frightening the younger children at school with scary ghost stories. But then Kirsty arrives. Kirsty claims that she can actually see ghosts – and she sees them in so many places that everyone becomes petrified. Then a mysterious virus sweeps through the school. Martin is still sure she is lying. After all, ghosts don't exist – do they?

Play... if you dare by Ruth Symes
Josie can hardly believe her luck when she finds the computer game at a car boot sale. "Play... if you dare," the game challenges. So she does. Further and further she plays, each level of the game scarier than the last. Then she reaches the last level. "Play... if you dare," repeats the game. But if she does, she could be trapped for ever...

All these books and many more can be purchased from your local bookseller. For more information about Tremors, write to: The Sales Department, Macdonald Young Books, 61 Western Road, Hove, East Sussex BN3 1JD.